MW01167580

DATE DUE
Fecha Para Retorn~

THE PROPOSITION

BRYAN FERRO

Vol. 2

H.M. Ward

www.SexyAwesomeBooks.com

Laree Bailey Press

AMAZON 3-30-15 8.00

COPYRIGHT

Laree Bailey Press
First Edition: Dec 2013
ISBN: 978-1-63035-012-3

CHAPTER 1

Bryan stands there with his jaw hanging open and those narrow, green eyes blazing. Fury and shock doesn't look good on him. The emotions contort his beautiful face, marring the smooth lines of his skin and making him look years older. His fingers ball into fists at his sides, but he blinks once and the reaction subsides. There are many things that I don't know about Bryan Ferro, but I do know this—he sucks at keeping things hidden. His thoughts dance across his face now and again, which is why he's leery of me.

Turning abruptly, Bryan presses his fingers to his right temple. His voice comes out like a growl. "I told you to leave." His shoulders are strained, every muscle is tight to the point that I can see the curves of his body under that dress shirt. He flexes the hand that's by his side before slipping it into his pocket. Bryan may be able to hide everything from everyone else, but not from me.

"Yeah, I heard that part." I act like I don't care, lay back on the carpet, and tuck my hands behind my head. The floor is soft and fuzzy. Lifting my knees, I let my gown fall around my ankles and scrunch up my feet to feel the soft pile between my toes. The carpet in my old room felt like a potato sack compared to this stuff. Even though Bryan's irate, I'm smiling. The little voice in the back of my head tells me that I've lost my mind. I answer back that I never really had a firm grip on it anyway.

Bryan can see my reflection in the mirror, but I can't see more than his back and the way he grips his head like it's going to explode. Is he that furious with me? I can't fathom his anger, but it pours out of his mouth again, barbed with thorns this time. "If you can't understand the terms of this agreement, then I'm afraid we don't have one."

"What?" I sit up and pivot around so I'm facing his back.

Bryan turns and the tension that's plastered across his face is horrible. I meet his gaze, but I can't hold it without wanting to fix whatever's doing this to him. All the pictures in the press show the version of Bryan that I knew—light and carefree—but this man is neither of those things. Something is crushing him from within and tearing him apart. His body is shaking, he's so angry. He tries to take a deep breath, but it just makes his face pinch tighter. "You heard me. If you don't do things my way, I'll ruin you. This is not my way, and you damn well know it. Get out."

He doesn't yell, but his words make me shiver. There's no warmth, no compassion. Maybe I don't know him anymore and he's right. Pressing my lips together, I swallow my retort, but it swells inside of me and fills my chest. I manage to get my heels back on my tired feet before standing. I walk over and grab my purse.

I should leave. The little voice inside of me chants like a pixie with a pleasant voice, *Yes, go. Do that. Now.*

My eyes are locked on the door like it's the pathway to Hell. Something about leaving right now feels wrong, but I can't put my finger on what's holding my feet in place. Damn, it's the thoughts that I'm holding back. They're trapping me here and I can't move. It feels like swallowing vomit and I can't do it. I'm brain damaged, but I can't be something I'm not.

Spinning on my foot, I cross the posh carpeted floor, and walk over to him. Bryan doesn't turn to look down at me. Instead, his hands are gripping the top of the bar like he wants to rip it out of the wall. His back is curved and his head is hung between his shoulders like he's trying not to tear me apart. Another woman would have run by now, but I'm the dopy one that walks closer.

"I'm a fool," I say while looking at my shoes, and laugh lightly. It's the kind of sound that has no joy and reveals a tortured soul. My eyes lift to his shoulders. I stand there for a moment waiting for him to turn, but he doesn't. Bryan doesn't speak or lift his gaze. He remains hunched over the bar like a troll.

I continue, "Seeing you tonight was terrifying and wonderful. It conjured memories and feelings that I'd long forgotten. Writing about it is one thing, but seeing you again is beyond words. I'm sorry I hurt you, even though I don't understand what I did. I'd fix it if I could. I'd…"

Why am I doing this? I'm begging to his back and the man doesn't even have the decency to turn and face me. I suck in and straighten my spine. "People make mistakes, Bryan, and it appears that my biggest mistake was meeting you."

Fury floods through me as I rush across the room. I grab the doorknob and don't look back even though I feel his eyes on me. Screw him. I've lived through worse. I chant those words over and over again, because I have. After scurrying down the hallway, I press the down button at the elevator bank over and over again, wondering why I'm so upset. After a moment, I feel the thought prick my eyes and take hold of my throat and I know exactly why I'm so upset.

It's possible that things are flipped around, and that I did not know the real Bryan Ferro—that the one from all those years ago, the one I slept with, was the fake.

CHAPTER 2

I can't go home and face Neil, so I call Maggie. She answers on the third ring. I'm walking on the street in front of the hotel with my phone pressed to my ear. It's late and dark. Avoiding the shadows, I walk closer to the street than the hotel. "Maggie." I try to hide the strain in my voice, but she hears it. We've known each other too long.

"I'll take his balls off. What the hell happened? Where are you?" She pelts me with questions until I can finally get her to shut up.

"I need a place to crash. I can't see Neil right now and I have nowhere else to go."

Maggie goes quiet. "What's mine is yours, you know that, but I'm not sure you'll like it."

"Anywhere is better than here or with Neil." I feel the warble work its way up my throat. Tears are coming, and from the feel of it, there's going to be a tidal wave.

"Sure, of course. I'll be there in five." Maggie's line goes dead and I tuck my phone into my purse.

The city moves around me, but it feels like I'm in a bubble. People pass on the sidewalk, but I fail to notice them. I pace, lost in thought, clutching my purse close to my body. The night air has that scent that is distinctly New York. I breathe it in and when I turn on my heel, I nearly slam into someone. The guy is a wall of brown and black. His coat smells like stale cigarettes and mothballs.

Before I have time to figure out what's happening, he grabs my purse, then places his hand on the center of my chest and shoves, hard. I scream and stumble back as my bag is ripped from my hands. The guy whirls around and is ready to take off, but I'm not about to lose that pocketbook. I'm fucking broke. All the money I have is in there.

Before I know what I'm doing, I take one of my heels and hurl it at his head. It connects and then drops to the sidewalk. A few people stop to watch, but no one does anything—typical New Yorkers. Everyone wants to see, but no one helps.

At that point everything happens in slow motion. I'm on my feet even though I don't remember standing. One foot is frozen, standing on the cold cement, while the other is still shoed. The thief lifts his hand to the back of his head and pulls it away. He glances at his fingers, his dark eyes taking in the sticky red blood on his hand. The edge of my heel connected with the back of his scalp, and must have nicked him.

My heart stops as the guy turns toward me. His eyes have a crazed look and his shoulders shake like he's going to rip me in half. "You." He says it like it's my name and he loathes me.

The man steps toward me and says it again, but his hands slowly drift upward, as if he's going to strike or strangle me. I gasp something, but it doesn't come out before I take a step back, terrified. My pulse roars in my ears as I look around for help, but don't see anyone. The crowd has walked off, or maybe I walked away. Where's a cop when I need one?

The rest happens frantically fast. Someone screams—me—as the man reaches for my neck. I drop, but he catches my shoulder. He shakes me hard, making my neck snap back and forth as he screams in my face. "You little bitch!"

The rest of his words turn to buzzing as he shakes me harder. I'm aware of the wind, the night air, and the man's strangle hold on me. At some point, his hands slide up to my neck. I claw at his hands and try to yell, but nothing comes out. I don't understand why no one sees us, why they just let this thief hurt me.

Swinging my legs, I kick at him, but it does no good. I'm not strong enough. I've tried everything I know to do and nothing works. The man hurls me around and slams my back against a brick wall. The cold jolts me and I wonder how we got to the alley next to the hotel, but those thoughts cease when I see the look in his eyes. An evil smile appears across his face as he tears the shoulder of my dress. The fabric comes away in his hand and lets the dress slip a few inches.

I open my mouth to scream, but his filthy hand covers it, sealing in the sound. His hand gropes me, feeling my breasts as he whispers in my ear all the horrible things he intends to do with me. "Then, I'll take my knife and—" His nasty words stop immediately after the sound of wood snapping.

Just as suddenly, the hand on my neck is gone and I gasp in a shaky breath and look up. It's too dark to see, but there's a man in a tux advancing on the thief. He throws punches over and over again until they're at the back of the alley, trapped by a brick wall. The thief is battered and bloody, but he doesn't stop fighting. Neither does the man in the tux. He throws punches like a boxer, so much so that it's hypnotic to watch. When that knife comes out, I expect things to turn in the thief's favor, but they don't. The man in the tux disarms the jackass and takes his weapon. It happened so fast that I can't tell how it was done. The man in the tux draws back his arm like he's going to push the knife through the guy's chest.

"Stop!" I call out before I realize what I'm doing. One of my hands is holding up my dress at the bustline and the other is barely touching my lips. I can't watch the guy die, but I can't look away either.

The man in the tux doesn't stop. A quivering cry is ripped from my throat as he slams the knife into the thief's shoulder. The thug grabs his arm and slides down the wall, gripping his shoulder as his coat gets soaked with blood. He looks straight at me with rage.

The man in the tux kicks the thief once, and a familiar voice says, "Leave."

I shiver when I hear it, because I know it's him—Bryan. He must have followed me. Fear grabs hold and sours inside my stomach as I stare at his back. Bryan doesn't turn to face me. The thief smashes his lips together and pushes up off the alley floor. He makes his way past me, and says nothing.

A tremor takes hold of me and drips down my spine, making me gasp. That's when he turns. Bryan's face is pale and covered in a thin sheen of sweat. He walks back toward me and I can see where he took a few hits. There's a tear in his shirt, under the lapel of his jacket, where the knife cut before Bryan got hold of it.

Step by step, he walks toward me and I'm more frightened by Bryan than anything I've encountered. What was that? Would he have killed the man if I didn't yell? I can't stop shaking.

Bryan reaches for my shoulders to steady me, and I feel that familiar jolt that goes with his touch. His thumb rubs softly over my skin. "Are you all right?"

But, it's too much. *I can't. I can't. I can't.* The thought makes no sense, but I know I have to get him to release me. His touch has a way of undoing me, and I'm falling apart. I refuse to let him be the one to witness it. I jerk away, and nod quickly. "I'm fine."

Bryan's hands remain frozen in the air for half a beat, before he lowers them along with his gaze. He watches the ground for a second and when he raises his chin a smirk is on his lips. "Liar. You're far from fine, but I'm glad you're still standing."

I stare at him, unable to come up with a response. His voice sounds affectionate, remorseful almost. He glances over my shoulder at someone and then says, "Your ride is here. Next time, don't try to take down a mugger by yourself."

I speak without meaning to, but the words bubble up and fall out. "Next time, don't kill a man for stealing my purse."

The corner of Bryan's lip tugs up, as if he wants to smile, but he doesn't. "I wouldn't kill a man for stealing a purse. What kind of person do you think I am?"

"I honestly don't know anymore. I thought I knew, but after this…" I shake my head and run out of words. Bryan changed his strike at the last second. That knife wasn't aimed at the man's shoulder— it was directed at his heart. "You were going to kill him. I saw, you can't tell me you weren't going to."

Bryan leans in close, and when he speaks his warm breath brushes against my ear. "Perhaps, but it wasn't because he took your bag." He leans back and slips both hands into his pockets as those green eyes slide over me. "No one touches you while you're with me." I swallow hard and stare at him with my heart still pounding.

Maggie appears behind me a second later. She grabs my shoulder and spins me around. "Hallie, what the hell is going on and why are you all the way back here by yourself?" She sees the way I'm clutching my gown and the torn fabric. Concern lingers on her face, waiting for my response.

"I'm not by myself," but when I turn to look, Bryan is gone.

CHAPTER 3

I've been in a cocoon of sorrow and this event broke it. My dazed indifference fractures and splinters like cheap glass. I stare at the purse clutched in my hand and wonder what's wrong with me, but even more so, I can't stop thinking about Bryan and how he came out of nowhere and nearly killed the man who tried to hurt me.

Stop thinking like that, I chide myself. Bryan acted like a lunatic. The image of Bryan stabbing the guy lights up behind my eyes again and makes my stomach churn.

Maggie's been talking, but I haven't said much. We're in her old Ford Escort. The thing barely runs, but I can't complain.

I don't even have a car, not anymore. Maggie glances over at me from behind the steering wheel while her hands grip it tightly. "Hallie, if you're going to hurl, put down the window. It smells weird enough in here." She's right, the car has an unidentifiable odor that's been there since she got it.

"I'm fine," I say again, although it's a lie. My arms are wrapped across my chest to hide how my hands tremble.

"Ah, Hallie, I know you don't want to talk and that's okay, but I don't want to put you over the top when you see my new place." I glance at her, not understanding what she means. Maggie gives me a sheepish smile and shrugs her shoulders into her ears as she drives. "Let's just say that it's not something you'd approve of."

I don't have the patience to deal with her riddles right now. Maggie's life is harder than mine and I know that, but she hasn't hidden things from me before. This time it's clear that she has, and it worries me. The only things I disapprove of are the ones likely to get her killed. The girl has no sense. Sometimes I wonder about her, and how she chooses what she does. I smile lamely and look at the grungy carpet on the once-blue floor.

"What's so funny?" Maggie looks indignant, as if I offended her.

"Nothing. Let's just say that if you knew what I was doing tonight, you wouldn't feel so defensive. I'm sure your place is fine."

Maggie's quiet. She sighs as she turns down a side street and we start to navigate our way through a dilapidated neighborhood. The houses are scarred and sun-bleached with dead lawns, but the cars are tricked out and costly. Even though it's late, people mill about, doing nothing. I glance at my door, wanting to lock it, but I don't move. As we roll past groups of people, their eyes turn and watch us pass, before they go back to whatever they were doing.

Maggie finally says, "It's not much, but I think it's worth it."

"You don't have to defend your apartment to me, Maggie. I'm freakin' homeless." I look over at her and tip my head back into the seat. My words don't comfort her, so I add, "Besides, I'm not the poster-child for morality either. You wouldn't believe what I did tonight, what I'm going to do." My voice trails off and I shake my head, thinking about Bryan's lips. I'm horrified that I react the way I do— even to the memory.

She laughs once, short. "Yeah, right. Hallie, you never do anything bad. Stupid, yes. Bad, no."

I stare out the window and look at nothing. The houses have given way to apartments that stretch up into the night sky. Their brick façade has seen better days. Many look empty, as if no one has lived there for years. My chest constricts and I squirm in my seat. My god, she lives here? Why didn't she tell me? There are burned out cars, overturned trash bins, and rubble strewn everywhere. It looks like the street was ransacked and forgotten—just like Maggie.

Spilt second decisions are the ones that change lives. I make mine and spit it out before I chicken out. "Bryan Ferro is blackmailing me. If I don't sleep with him whenever he wants, he's going to tell people that he's the guy in the book and do whatever it takes to ruin me. He said he'd use everything he has against me and gave me an ultimatum."

Maggie's big eyes turn toward me with her jaw dangling wide open. "Holy shit! When did this happen? How are you going to stop him?" She blinks at me and turns her eyes back to the road, even though I know she doesn't want to.

This is the part that makes me feel like crap. I'm not who she thinks I am. I don't have a moral spine of steel. I can't even look at her. "Tonight. I ended up doing the award show announcement with him, and then he found me at the banquet." *Say it.* I try to make my mouth move to form the words, but they won't come out.

"No fucking way." She pulls into a parking lot that looks like it was used as an air force blast site and turns off her car. "Grab all your stuff and lock the door." I do as she says and hurry behind her. "Keep your eyes to yourself and follow me up. Don't talk to anyone."

We enter the side of one of those old brick buildings and take a few flights of stairs up to the fourth floor. By the time we reach her landing, I want to throw my remaining shoe out the window. I could, there's no glass in the pane. I follow her through the door and down a long, poorly lit hallway. We stop at front of her door. While she fumbles for the key, the door across from her opens. A pale man with bleach-blonde hair in a wife-beater shirt and boxer shorts stands there and looks us over. I can feel his eyes on my back. He leans against the doorjamb and folds his arms over his chest.

When he speaks, he sounds raspy, like he's smoked a carton of cigarettes every day since he was two years old. "Brought me another one?"

"No," Maggie says sternly. She doesn't turn around to look at the guy. If I didn't know better, I'd think she was afraid of him. I can't take more stress tonight. My brain feels like it's going to break in two before it shrivels up and dies. Maggie gets the key to turn but the door sticks. She kicks it once with her foot and it budges slightly. "Damn door," she mutters.

"What's your name, sweet thing?" The guy is speaking to me. I turn and look over my shoulder, and our eyes meet. It sends a chill through me to see the way he's leering at me. The guy is a rail, but he's all muscle and right now he's smiling at me, revealing a golden crown on his eyetooth.

"Hi," I say shyly, and tuck my hair behind my ear, attempting to avoid his gaze while not answering his question.

Just as the guy's mouth opens, Maggie kicks in the door. It flies open, she grabs my arm, and tugs. I follow, flying along after her as she yells over her shoulder, "I'll bring you someone tomorrow, I swear. Goodnight, Vic." She slams the door shut with her foot and looks shaken.

Her apartment is about the same size as a short hallway. There's a tiny window with a sheet stapled over it and no furniture. Some of Maggie's clothes are thrown around the place, like she left in a hurry. If I lived here, I'd leave quickly, too. "Thanks for letting me stay with you."

"Yeah, no problem. It sucks, as in this is the worst place I've ever lived, but it's shelter. I sleep here and then get the hell out. The rent isn't horrible." She offers a crooked smile, but it's weak.

I need her, and there's a wall between us. She thinks that I'm perfect, but I'm not. I've done things that she doesn't know about. The words are on my tongue and I roll them around in my mouth, trying to figure out how to say it as Maggie chatters, filling the air with her voice.

A couple is fighting nearby, and the sound is growing louder. And by fighting, I don't mean arguing. There are things hitting walls and crashing. Plaster rains down on us like snowflakes when something else crashes overhead. Maggie looks horrified as she pulls her murphy bed down from the wall. It takes up nearly the entire room. "You can sleep here. I'll take the floor."

"No."

She smiles. "Don't be silly, you're my guest." Choice words ring out from above us as an angry man hollers. It's promptly followed by a high pitched scream. Maggie bites her nails the way she did when we were kids and looks around, as if she wishes she could torch the place.

"I'm not making you sleep on the floor, but there's something else that I need to tell you." Maggie looks up at me from under her mass of red hair. I'm her only real friend, her only family—and she's mine. God, what is she going to think of me when I tell her what I agreed to? I don't think I'll be able to stand it. My arms are still folded over my chest, with my hands nestled tightly into the crooks of my arms.

"Hallie, what's wrong?" Maggie stops making the bed and sits. She pats the spot next to her and I sit down.

Staring straight ahead, I swallow hard and tell her. "I said yes."

"You said yes to what? Hallie, you're not making sense, what are you talking about?"

When I turn to look at her, I meet those big green eyes and feel afraid. My skin covers in goose bumps, but I can't look away. "I told Bryan Ferro yes. I caved. He won and I lost."

"What?" She's livid, ready to fly out of her seat and defend me to the death.

I place my hand on her lap to still her. "I went to his hotel room to tell him to

THE PROPOSITION 2

suck it, but I changed my mind when I heard his voice. I thought that something was wrong and this was his crappy way of telling me. I knew him once, at least I thought I did. Then, when I was waiting for you outside, I—" my voice is shaking and I can no longer hide my horror, "some guy tried to steal my purse. Long story short, he got me behind the building and was going to hurt me. Bryan showed up and he…" I can't say it. My perfect Bryan did something that was so unlike him, so horribly savage that I don't know what to think. He protected me, but it still feels wrong.

"Did he hurt you?" Maggie is furious, I can hear it in her voice. The way it's too loud and her words are too staccato gives her away.

"No, he attacked the man, and stabbed him. If I didn't tell Bryan to stop, I think he would have killed the guy." I glance over at her, but I can no longer see. My eyes have the pre-tears sheen that makes the world go blurry.

Maggie lifts her arms and I fall into them. She's always been like a sister to me. We've been there for each other, and I'm afraid this mess with Bryan will make her hate me and what I've become. My father would have been ashamed to call me his daughter, and I expect the same from Maggie. Instead, she sits there on the worn mattress and soothes me.

After one hard hug, she releases my shoulders and grabs my chin. "You and I have been through everything together. Don't think that I'm bailing because of this. If anything, life just got more interesting, that's all."

I wipe the tears from my eyes and laugh, because she's so wrong. "That's the understatement of the year."

"My point is, I'm here for you. I'll always be here for you." She bumps my shoulder with hers. "So, Bryan Ferro has a dark side behind all that flash and dazzle?"

"Apparently."

"Was it fun or did he do weird stuff?"

I smile and wipe my eyes again. "No, not tonight anyway. He called me to his room, I went, and we kissed. Then, he threw me out."

Maggie's lip pull up a little. "He threw you out? What the hell?"

"I don't know. It's like he was mad and going to Hulk-out or something. He wouldn't look at me. Things were hot and heavy until then." Intuition keeps telling me that something was wrong, but I can't put my finger on what.

Maggie grins, "He was better than Neil, right?"

I make a face and look at her like she's nuts. "Uh, Bryan's blackmailing me."

"And he's hotter than Neil. Go on, say it. I'm your friend, so I already know."

I cast my eyes toward the floor and don't say anything. I don't have to, my expression says everything. Bryan is so much hotter than Neil that there is no comparison. The two men are night and day, and Bryan is the sexy night. Neil's the rational voice that sounds like the FDA reminding me to do all things in moderation—but not all things—only the actions he approves of. Damn it. I bury my face in my hands and sigh.

Maggie pats my back once. "It's okay. Every guy is hotter than Neil. Don't feel guilty, but I wouldn't exactly tell Mr. Perfectly Pressed Pants. He'll freak out that someone else touched you." Maggie is pulling off her clothes and tugging on a night shirt and sweat pants as she speaks.

"Actually, Neil knows."

"What?" She's hopping on one foot, trying to shove her foot into the hole and falls over. "How does he know? You said it just happened."

"Neil knows because he's the one who told me to do it."

CHAPTER 4

Maggie has only gone totally nuclear
once. It was when we got split up from a
foster home when we were seven. Within
three days, they had us back together under
the same roof. Maggie would never say
what she did, only that she went nuke-crazy
and launched everything she had at them.
The look in her eyes says she wants to hand
Neil his balls in a Dixie cup.

Maggie rocks upright with her pants
half on and half off as her jaw locks tight.
She looks away from me and cracks her
neck, like she's going to kill someone.

When she swings her green eyes back my way, there's a pleasant, yet terrifying, smile on her face. When she speaks, she sounds cordial, like someone who works in a lovely flower shop and loves people—in other words—she sounds totally demented. "He told you to go?" She laughs lightly and flutters her lashes at me as she tips her head to the side. "And he knew you were being blackmailed?"

I don't want to talk about it. I'm so tired that I'm going to start drooling on myself soon. "Yeah, he knew." I don't want to tell her the rest. As it is, she's already three stages passed livid.

"What wonderful reason did he give, because it must have been good?" She clasps her hands calmly, but I know there's an eruption ready to explode beneath the cool façade.

I rub my eyes hard and tug at my dress zipper, but it seems caught in the fabric. "Maggie, put your PJs on and go to sleep. I don't want to talk about it. Obviously I'm mad at Neil or I wouldn't be here with you."

She studies me for a moment, those suspicious eyes narrowing, before saying, "But Neil doesn't realize you're upset, and you want him to think that Bryan Ferro nailed you." Her eyebrow lifts when I glance at her. It's her I-know-what-you're-thinking face.

Unfortunately, she realizes exactly what I'm thinking, but that doesn't make me want to discuss it. Neil shouldn't have offered me up like that. It felt like he abandoned me when I needed him. I have issues with that particular topic, which makes me constantly second guess myself—but not this time. I wouldn't have done this to him. I wouldn't have made him sleep with someone for money. Damn, that makes me sound like a prostitute.

Pressing my eyes closed, I look away. "Maybe."

Perhaps Neil should suffer a little for being so callous, because that's what it was—indifference. At the same time, before tonight ever happened, Neil handed me my life back. The guy was an anchor when the shore was far out of sight. He was there for me in my darkest hours and part of me feels guilty for being here with Maggie, even though I know I shouldn't. Sometimes I wish I didn't feel anything. It seems like life would be easier.

At the moment, Maggie's emotions are smeared across her face like molten crayons. "Holy shit, Hallie! Why are you with him? Neil came along and picked you up when you were—"

I cut her off. "I know what I was, and maybe Neil was in the right place at the right time, but he's never done anything like this before, and neither have I. I kept this from him." I lied to him, over and over again.

"And he's kept stuff from you! Would you have made him do something he didn't want to do?" She pauses, and adds, "You didn't want to see Ferro again, did you?"

I shake my head and look away. She's right. There's no way that I would have made Neil do something like this, but he didn't really give me a choice. I had no choice, not if I wanted to get on with my life. There's too much money at stake. Holding up my hand, I say, "I don't want to talk about it anymore tonight."

Maggie makes an annoyed sound in the back of her throat and continues to get dressed. After she pulls on her sweats, she goes over to a rust-stained sink and brushes her teeth. While foaming at the mouth, she turns and looks at me and jabs the toothbrush toward me. "You know I'd kick ass for you. Just tell me who and I'm there." On the last word, toothpaste foam goes flying from her lips.

I offer a half smile. "I know you would, but I don't know who pissed me off more—Neil or Bryan."

Maggie tosses me a nightshirt and continues talking, but my mind is reeling. I'm mad at Neil, but Bryan—I don't know. The way he spoke, the way his voice caught in his throat when he said certain things, it's almost like he didn't want to do it—but he did—he blackmailed me.

He didn't sleep with you. He kissed you and threw you out, that inner-voice chimes inside my head like a clock.

Bryan's words didn't match his actions, and if he didn't drive that knife into the thief's shoulder, I would have thought the man I saw tonight was my Bryan from years ago, but that wasn't him. Whatever's happened to Bryan between then and now has changed him, and although the new man saved me, he frightens me.

CHAPTER 5

The night passes slowly as it always does. I hear my father's voice although he is no longer here. My memories are stuck on rewind, repeating random things as they fly to the front of my mind. It haunts me until I can no longer bear it.

Maggie is snoring a few feet from my head. I rock, paper, scissored her for the bed and she won. We made up a small pallet on the floor for me, but it's more like a blanket and a sheet. They're tangled from my tossing and turning. I push them aside and sit up, rubbing my stinging eyes. Maggie's old clock glows softly next to her bed. It's almost 6am.

My body aches like I was shoved down an elevator shaft, but I push myself off the floor and head over to her narrow window. The shouts that filled the building last night have grown quiet. The woman overhead cried out one last time a few hours ago, and then something heavy hit the floor. I wonder if one of them is dead. The sounds that make my skin crawl have receded into silence.

I lean against the wall and wrap my arms around my middle as I gaze out the narrow, hazy window. The sun is yet to spill over the horizon and the city is still painted in darkness. The sidewalks below are mostly empty. The groups of people standing in clusters have dissolved. The figures in the shadows are gone.

Sometimes I wonder if the monsters in my mind are worse than the ones on the street. I came from the streets, so did Maggie. We survived so much and yet, I can't escape the memories that haunt me night after night. Add my father's death to the mix and I'm a walking time bomb. I wish I could say I know who I am and that the events of my past didn't change me, but

I can't even imagine my life without those occurrences. If my mother hadn't left me alone, if she didn't do what she did, what kind of woman would I be? If she was a good person and raised me, where would we be now?

I swallow hard and force the questions away. They serve no purpose and will only pull me backward. I fought so hard to get away from that life, but it lives forever in the back of my mind. I hear her voice and the familiar slurred speech. I remember the sting of her hand on my cheek and too many nights spent shivering in a dark closet, while she lived a life that didn't consider me. Most parents want to protect their children, but not my mom. She didn't want me. She lived for herself and that's the one thing that frightens me most—that I'll become her.

My fingers tighten into my sides as I try not to shudder, because the apartment is freezing. God, this place reminds me of that past life. I don't know how Maggie can stand it. I glance over at her and think about the things I could do for us if I had that money. I could save her from this—

But who will save you? The little voice in my head whispers.

Dad won't come and rescue me this time. This time the only way out of this mess is through Bryan Ferro. I've endured more hardships than most people see in a lifetime, I can survive whatever he wants to dish out—I just don't know if I'll like the woman I become because of it.

Some things aren't worth the price. I've learned that firsthand, and now here I am, repeating my mother's actions.

I grit my teeth and mutter under my breath, "I'm not the same...it's not the same thing."

My gaze falls to the window sill and I instinctively lean toward it, pressing my fingertips against the cold glass. I don't understand what I'm seeing at first. Someone is standing in the shadow of the building across the way. They're inside a room, a floor down from where I stand in Maggie's building, across the street. The person is a silhouette with no defining characteristics. I think it's a woman, but I'm not certain. She's stepping backward slowly. Her hands lift, like a dog is about to pounce on her stomach. Suddenly, her spine goes straight and she stops moving. The window is so narrow that I can't see much more than her slender figure through the gauzy drapes.

A moment later she goes limp and falls forward. Her hair cascades behind her, falling in slow motion. I hear nothing but Maggie's nasal breaths, but her silent scream is ringing in my ears. A taller form—a man—steps into the spot where the woman once stood. His shoulders are rounded, like he's not worried about a thing, as he shakes his head and surveys the floor like there's something amusing.

My throat tightens as I watch in horror, frozen in place. At that moment, the man looks up and glances out the window. Our eyes lock and time stops as an unseen force steals my breath. The hairs on the back of my neck prickle as I stare, unable to look away.

Maggie told me to keep my eyes down and not say a damn thing to anyone, but I can't, and even worse—I recognize him and his bright blonde hair. It's the man who lives across the hall.

CHAPTER 6

I'm not sure if he realizes who he's looking at, but I'm certain that he knows which apartment we're in. Heart racing, I spin on my heel and stumble into Maggie's bed. "Get up." My voice is choked, and barely comes out. Frantically, I shake her awake. "We need to leave. Now."

Maggie pushes up on her elbows. Make-up is smeared across the right side of her face. She looks like a weeping clown. "What?" She's too groggy and we don't have time for it.

"Move. Now." I issue one word commands and toss a pair of jeans at her and start gathering anything important. I'm shaking so much that I drop the armload of items and my purse spills out on the floor. Maggie stops asking what's wrong. She's caught my mood and glances at the door like she already knows.

Suddenly, she's awake and moving like she chugged a case of energy shots. "What'd you see? Fuck, Hallie! I told you not to look at anything." I can't believe she's scolding me, but I'm not going to waste time arguing with her.

Kneeling, I pull all the clothing and purse contents into my arms. "Go, go, go!" I head to the door, leaving my evening gown behind. We race down the hall half-dressed and stampede down the stairs. I toss everything into the backseat of Maggie's car and jump into the front. "Go!"

Maggie shoves the key in the ignition and the engine turns over. She grips the wheel firmly and pulls away. For a second, I think we made it, that we'll escape unnoticed, but just as we reach the end of the block, I look back in the side view mirror. The man from across the hall is watching our taillights as we drive away.

CHAPTER 7

"What did you see?" Maggie yells again, as she looks back in the mirror. Her eyes widen, but she doesn't blink. She glances at him as he sees us drive away. "Fuck, are you serious? That's Victor! Why is he watching us? We don't want him watching us! Hallie, what happened?" Maggie's voice goes up an octave from the time she starts talking to the time she finishes.

"His name is Victor?"

"Yes! Victor Campone. He's fucking crazy!" Maggie's body is stiff and I can tell that it's taking a lot of effort not to floor it and flee. She doesn't want to draw attention to us, so she goes at a normal speed even though it feels like my heart is going to explode.

"He killed someone." My voice is soft, barely audible. My stomach is twisting like I ate something rancid. Swallowing makes the queasy feeling worse, so I lean my head back and press my fingers to my face.

"No, no, no! Tell me you didn't see anything!"

"I saw it. He was in the apartment across from us. I was looking out the window."

"And he saw you?" I nod and rub the heel of my hand into my eyes. Maggie's voice picks up a quiver that is so unlike her that it scares me. "He doesn't know you saw a thing, right? I mean, it's not like he was watching you while he did it. We didn't see anything. We don't know anything. Everything will be fine." She starts rambling, more to herself than me.

"Who is he?"

"No one. He's no one. You don't know that name, you never saw his face." Maggie's knuckles have turned white from gripping the wheel so hard. "We didn't pull out and fly down the street, so it looks like I was just taking you home."

After a while we make it to my neighborhood. Maggie pulls up in front of Neil's apartment and shuts off the car. "I'll go back later and act like nothing happened. It'll be fine."

"The hell you will! You can't live like that Maggie." What has she gotten herself into? Sympathy crosses my face before I can hide it, which pisses her off.

"Don't look at me like that. I can take care of myself."

"No, not this time. This time you made a mistake. That guy is insane. How do you know he didn't kill some lady like you? How do you know you won't be next?" She doesn't look at me, instead Maggie acts like she didn't hear me at all. "Maggie how do you know!"

Turning, she snaps, "I don't know, all right! No one knows when their time is up or how they're going to die, and neither do I! Leave it alone, Hallie. You messed up enough things already. I can fix it."

"No, you can't! This isn't stuff that can be fixed!" I'm yelling at her, and I can't stop. My heart is racing so fast that it's slamming into my ribs and my hands are shaking. "Your death waits in that building! Every time you walk in there, your life expectancy drops. You can't seriously think that it has no ramifications. He killed someone! The couple above you beat the crap out of each other until one of them fell on the floor. Do you need to wait until you're the one who is dead on the floor to see that you're not safe?"

"I have no choice!" She's breathing hard and fast like me. I want to cry and save her from all of this, but I can't. A moment passes where neither of us speaks.

I tip my head back against the seat and glance over at her. "What do you do for him?"

"I can't tell you." Maggie doesn't look at me. Instead, she stares blankly ahead.

"Who is he?"

"You don't want to know." I open my mouth to press her, but she holds up a single finger and gives me a stern look. "Don't. Knowing will only bring you more trouble."

I don't like it, but I stop asking. I wish so much that things weren't like this. I have to get the money from the book deal. I need it, for her. She's in over her head, and the horrible part is, so am I.

CHAPTER 8

Maggie follows me into the house after grabbing all of our stuff from her car. After I've showered, I head to the kitchen and find Neil waiting at the table. He's reading the paper like he's not upset in the slightest. He folds it and places it on the table before looking up at me. "So, how'd it go?"

"Fine." My jaw is tight. I can barely spit out the words. I want to bite his head off, but if I do that I'll be homeless. When did I turn into such a spineless wimp? *Whore, Hallie. The word you're looking for is whore.* I don't want to think about it, so I grab a coffee cup from the cabinet and take my time pouring the hot liquid, so I don't have to look at him.

Before I know what's happening, Neil is walking toward me. I think he's going to fight, but his voice is timid. "I shouldn't have made you do it. I'm sorry, Hallie." I can feel his eyes on my back and the pleading tone in his voice makes my heart break.

"No, you shouldn't have," is all I can manage. I keep my eyes focused on the black liquid in my cup, watching the steam rise from the surface.

"Listen, I thought—from the way you two were acting on stage—I thought you still liked him."

His confession catches me off guard. I turn slowly and look over my shoulder at him. Is he serious? For some reason it feels like I'm being played, but I dismiss it. How jaded am I? The guy's trying to apologize and I want something safe right now. Neil is the epitome of safe.

For a moment, I can't speak. Then I manage a, "I don't." My words are noncommittal. I was going to say I don't have feelings for him, but I do. I feel something for Bryan, but I don't know what it is. Fear? Lust? Attraction doesn't mean anything anyway, does it?

Neil nods once and watches his feet. His sandy hair obscures his eyes. "So, you forgive me?"

"If you can forgive me?" Where'd that come from? The words shock me, but that doesn't stop them from coming from my mouth. I shouldn't have to ask him to pardon me for past lovers, for things that happened before I knew him, but I just did.

His lips pull into a soft smile. "I already have. I understand why you didn't say anything about him. I mean, it's embarrassing, right? You didn't want to make things weird between us by mentioning that. People have dark spots in their pasts, and he's yours. I got it. I'm sorry I pushed you back there, and I'm so glad you came home again. I thought I might have lost you." Neil holds up his arms, like he wants a hug.

I put down my mug and fall into his arms. Neil holds me like I'm fragile, and gently kisses my cheek. We stay like that for a moment, until a voice breaks us apart.

"I should have clarified the terms of my silence." Bryan is standing in front of us in the doorway between the living room and the kitchen. "There's to be no intimacy of any kind between you two, while Hallie is with me and I'm not done with her yet."

CHAPTER 9

Neil releases me and steps away. His jaw drops half way open and he does a double take, like he can't believe Bryan had the audacity to walk into his home. "You have no right to be here."

Bryan grins and slips his hands into his pockets. He's wearing dark jeans and a fitted T-shirt that reveals his delicious body. A worn leather jacket hangs from his shoulders and his hair is still damp, like he just rolled out of bed.

"Do I smell coffee?" Bryan ignores Neil, shoves past us, and grabs my cup off the counter. "Still drinking it black, huh, Hallie?" He winks at me, before gulping down my drink.

"Holy shit." Maggie appears with dripping wet hair and her jaw dragging on the floor. Her eyes dart between Neil and Bryan like she's anticipating an explosion.

Bryan leans back on the counter, which makes his jacket open, revealing more of his toned chest and that clingy shirt. When he grins, he seems like the old Bryan, complete with a lickable dimple. "Hey Red," he nods toward Maggie with his magical smile.

"Hey yourself." Maggie laughs, and looks over at me and then Neil.

Neil looks appalled and remains frozen for a few seconds before he puffs up, angry. "Get out or I'll call the police."

Bryan shrugs like he doesn't care and doesn't move. "Go ahead. You call them and I'll call my friends, and get things rolling." He pulls his cell phone from his pocket and holds it up. "Well, go on."

Neil glances at me and then Bryan. "You said one night."

"Yeah, I changed my mind. Last night didn't go as planned, and I figured why not ask for more? If you say no, you lose everything. It's kind of a no-brainer, so I went for it." Bryan speaks to Neil, but he's watching Maggie when he talks.

After resting my empty mug on the counter, Bryan walks over to me. "Ready?"

"You said you'd call." My hands are balled at my sides and I wish I was taller so I could yell at Bryan eye to eye.

He offers a typical Bryan Ferro grin and shrugs. "Yeah, I'm whimsical like that. I thought I'd drop by and pick you up. Besides, I needed to make sure that your douche boyfriend doesn't touch you."

"These weren't the terms. You cannot change your demands like this." Neil is agitated, but Maggie leans against the doorjamb with an amused look on her face. Neil inhales slowly, trying to keep his temper under wraps, but it's there, brewing, and Bryan is stoking the fire.

"Actually, I can. It goes with the whole agreement we made last night, right Hallie?" Bryan watches me for a second and then adds, with false sincerity, "Oh, I'm sorry, you didn't get a chance to tell him yet?"

"Bryan." I warn, but he doesn't stop.

He walks over next to me and drapes his arm over my shoulders. "Last night I told her that one night wasn't enough. Sorry, I thought you already knew, and it's not like it'd matter to you anyway because it's all the same. I slept with her before, so what's one more night, right?" Bryan's voice turns razor sharp as he says the last few words. He releases me and steps toward Neil, so they're close enough to punch each other. "You did say something to that effect, didn't you?"

Neil squares his shoulders. He won't be told off by a Ferro. He thinks Bryan's a spoiled brat and gives him the most condescending look I've ever seen. "It's not like you to want a woman more than once. Doesn't that go against the Ferro code of honor-less actions? I've heard your sister—"

Before Neil can finish the sentence, Bryan's arm darts out. He grabs Neil by the throat and hisses, "If you value your life, you won't finish that sentence." Bryan's twin sister seems to catch bad press way too often, which is horrible because she's really sweet. They never run that kind of story though, it's always stuff about the Ferro heiress and her brainless, chasteless actions.

Bryan tightens his grip and then releases. Neil sucks in air and rubs his throat, but doesn't look away. I want to scream at Bryan, but I don't. Instead, I ask, "What do you want, Bryan?"

His green eyes drift back my way and his gaze softens. "You."

He says it like I'm all he wants in the world, but I know that's not true. I'm what he wants right now, for punishment or pleasure, I'm still not sure. Bryan holds out his hand. "Come on, I have our day planned."

I glance at Neil, but he won't look at me. For a second, I think about saying no, but Maggie is standing there smiling. I want to keep that happy expression on her face and to do that I need money. Taking Bryan's hand, I slip my fingers into his warm grip.

CHAPTER 10

I'm sitting across from Bryan in a little booth at a Friendly's restaurant, out of all places. The irony doesn't escape me. This is where happy people come to have food and ice cream, not deranged Ferro men and their blackmailed friends, or whatever I am.

Poking at a fry, I finally ask, "What are we doing here?"

Bryan hasn't made any mention of sex since we left Neil's this morning. Before we'd gone, I told Maggie to stay put, but she won't. I know her. She'll go back home after work and act like nothing happened and it's going to get her killed. I'd been hoping Bryan would do what he wanted and toss me out again so I could stop her. I poke at the ketchup, before dropping the fry.

Bryan doesn't answer right away. He has that casual smile he wears on his face like life is so fun and he can't get enough. Sometimes I want to slap it away. How can he act like nothing matters? He's not the man I remember.

He flashes his green gaze at me before grinning that beautiful smile that makes a small dimple appear on his cheek. I remember tracing the lines of his face with my tongue years ago, and paying extra attention to that little spot. It's like he knows, because the slant of his mouth changes as if he's thinking dirty thoughts. "We're having lunch."

"I know that, but is this seriously why you picked me up this morning? Because you didn't want to eat alone?"

He pops a fry into his mouth and nods. The movement makes his dark hair fall over his brow. He sweeps it back with his hand and tips his head to the side while pointing a new fry at me. "You hate eating alone."

"That's not the point."

"Then, what is the point?"

"This wasn't supposed to be a date! Sex, Bryan, you said you wanted sex and that's it." I whisper-yell at him, leaning across the table, but it doesn't stop the waitress from choosing that moment to reappear.

Her eyes go wide as the grumpy expression on her face vanishes and is replaced by an amused and somewhat interested look. "Need anything else, hun? Well, anything that I can get you?" Bryan nearly spews his milkshake as my face turns cherry red. The waitress looks me over and then winks at me before she walks away.

Bryan is practically choking, but finally manages to speak. "Can we add her to the agreement? I think she's into you." His body shakes as he tries to repress his laughter and fails.

I've slumped forward to hide my face at the same time I've slid down in the booth. Someone, shoot me. I kick Bryan under the table. "I want to leave."

"Yes, you said that already. All good things come in time." My lips are drawn together, trying not to say the line running through my head. Bryan and I used to banter so well, but I don't want this. It's not real. He's extorting me. I wouldn't be here if he wasn't. "Oh, come on, Hallie. I know you want to say it. Just say it. Be you and stop acting like the repressed version of yourself that your boyfriend turned you into."

"I'm not discussing Neil with you."

"Yeah, because there's nothing to discuss."

"I hate you."

"Yeah, you said that already."

The waitress walks past and drops a check on the table. Bryan picks it up and chuckles. "Want her number?" He holds up the tab and shows me her handwritten message on the top: *Call me XOXO* followed by her number.

I make an aggravated sound and shove out of the booth. We have to get on with things so I can stop Maggie. I can't be in two places at once. I wish Bryan would just get on with things, but he doesn't. I try to walk out of the restaurant without him, but he grabs a belt loop on my jeans and tugs me back to him as we walk outside into the crisp air.

Then his arm is around my waist. He's walking next to me and whispering in my ear, "Got some place to be?"

"No, you're the only person who I'm whoring myself out to today." He flinches and his hand slips from my side. I continue to walk, not noticing that he's stopped. When I turn back, Bryan is watching me and I can tell that there's a war waging within him. He knows damn well what he's done to me, but he did it anyway.

"You're not a whore." The wind whips the hair out of his eyes as he stands there, unblinking. His voice is calm, even.

The corner of my mouth tugs up into a sad smile and I shake my head. "I know what I am, what I have to do, and I already said yes. I am what you made me, so let's not sugarcoat things. I don't want to pretend."

"I do." His confession surprises me.

My lips part, but I don't know what to say, so I stand there gaping at him. A car pulls into the parking lot and drives between us. Neither of us moves, we just stand there frozen with unspoken thoughts. He looks away and takes a shaky breath before that playful smirk returns to his face. It's his mask, a guise that hides every thought in his head, so no one will ever know what he really thinks or feels about anything.

I hate it. I want him to throw it away, but I don't dare ask. The guy I knew isn't in there anymore. He can't be. I step toward him and look up into his face. The pull between us is strong and I know I'll regret this, but I say it anyway. "Then, let's pretend. I'll be me and you be you. No time has passed, we never broke up, you don't hate me—oh, and you didn't threaten me. I'm here because I want to be. I'll be her, I'll be the version of me that you remember, because that's what you want, isn't it? I wrote about the past, but you want to relive it, so we will."

Bryan studies my face as I speak, his eyes lock with mine and don't look away. "And?"

"And you will act like the man you are now and stop this fake crap."

Bryan's chest rises and falls as his eyes drift to my dark hair. He lifts a curl and winds it around his finger, studying the smoothness of my dark strands like he's never done so before. "You don't want that."

"Uh, no, you don't want that. Bryan…" my voice trails off. I'm so frustrated. Butterflies are swirling in my stomach and I swear to God that they're going to fly out of my nose if I don't either kiss him or step away, but I can't. We're locked together like two pieces of a puzzle. I drop my eyes and suck in a jagged gulp of air. Bryan's gaze heats my face, slowly caressing it, relearning the lines and curves that were once so familiar to him.

"Hallie." I look up when he calls my name and before I know what's happened his hands are on my cheeks and his lips are pressed to mine. It's the softest kiss I've ever felt, gentle as a snowflake's caress. It leaves me shaking and craving more, but he's pulled away.

Bryan's lips are parted as he watches me. He finally says, "Things are this way for a reason. Trust me when I say that you don't want to know more."

Bitterness chokes me. "Trust you. That's rich."

"I trust you." Damn, those eyes. They penetrate me to my core, stealing glimpses of my soul. His expression is so sincere that it scares me.

I give a knee-jerk reaction and counter, "You shouldn't. You don't know me anymore, and as soon as I get the chance, I'll get even with you for this. I swear to God, I will."

I mean every word I say. Vengeance burns through me and a steady stream of heat makes my fingers curl at my sides. Despite the attraction, I can sense when someone is out to hurt me and I know— without a doubt—that Bryan will decimate me. I feel the sensation swirl within my gut, warning me to stay away.

The luminous smile returns to his beautiful face before he clicks his tongue and raises a brow at me. Leaning in close to my face, he whispers, "I'm looking forward to it."

CHAPTER 11

I need liquor. Seriously. My heart has been pounding since that kiss and it won't slow down. The constant adrenaline rush is making me frantic. I want to run, scream, and dance all at the same time. Manic laughter tries to bubble up from within me, but I grip my hands together and twist, trying to force it back down.

Bryan, on the other hand, seems completely cool and collected. We're laying on the lawn behind the mansion at the Bayard Cutting Arboretum. There's an enormous grassy field that stretches from the back of the house all the way down to the water. Lavish houses line the opposite shore, but none are as large as this one. It's one of the oldest homes in the area and it was turned into a state park before I can remember. There aren't many people outside today, it's a bit too brisk, but Bryan doesn't mind and neither do I.

We lay in the grass, side by side, and stare at the sky. Bryan's hands are tucked behind his head revealing the toned body that I used to know so well. But he's older now and the lines of his chest and waist have changed. Rather than growing softer, he's become more angular with a trimmer waist. The muscles in his arms curve perfectly. The thought of having those arms around me flashes through my mind, but I swat the thought away. Eventually, he'll stop playing and demand what he wants, but for now Bryan is content to stare at clouds and pretend we're friends.

After a prolonged silence he confesses, "When I was a kid I wanted to live here. I thought I could buy this house." He laughs softly and glances over at me. "That was the first time I learned that some things can't be bought."

I don't respond because his admission gets under my skin. Apparently he can't buy a house, but he can buy me. I press my lips together and stare at a cloud that's all fluffy, curvy lines.

Bryan's eyes are on the side of my face, but I don't look at him. When I do, I get lost in the depths of him and only see what I want to see. I wish so badly that we remained friends, but things didn't turn out that way, and now here we are, with me plotting to get even with him on the lawn of one of our old hang outs. Yeah, we were weird. Bryan and I used to walk around here when we were together. The only other people around are the elderly and flocks of geese and ducks that reside down by the water.

When he looks away, Bryan takes a deep breath, and asks, "Why'd you write it about me? I mean, you could have written anything you wanted about any of your lovers and you chose me. I want to know why." He has trouble asking the question. The way his voice comes out tells me so.

"I don't want to talk about it anymore. Besides, I already told you. It wasn't meant to offend anyone." Screw that, it wasn't meant to be seen by anyone. I have horrible luck. For every good thing that happens, three more sucky things pop up at the same time. Bryan is a clusterfuck of payback for my good fortune.

I steal a glance his way when he doesn't answer. His dark lashes are closed and he's breathing deeply, like my response pained him. When his eyes open again, he sees me. Bryan rolls onto his side and we're nose to nose. "I don't care if this whole thing blows up in my face, it's worth the price." I say nothing as my pulse pounds harder and his lips draw nearer. His emerald eyes dip from my gaze to my lips and back. In a low voice he says, "Pretend you love me. Kiss me, Hallie... Just once."

Those words take hold of my heart and rip it from my chest. How can he say things like that to me? After everything we've been through, after the way he's been treating me. I steady my voice, not trusting it to come out as sternly as I need it to. "You have no right to say things like that to me."

"Don't you wish for things, Hallie? Don't you dream of second chances?"

He's plunged a dagger into my heart and is twisting it. I might as well be the thief from last night because his words are killing me. I realize what bothers me most about all of this and it's crippling—I never stopped loving him. It didn't matter that we parted ways and never spoke again, my affection didn't die. It's still there, burning bright and he knows. I can't protect myself from him, I've never been able to mask my emotions from him.

My words turn to ice and I steel my voice, "There is no such thing as a second chance. Ask my mother or my father— whoever he is. Ask the man who adopted me and spared me from so much for so long. Ask me why I don't wish or want anymore. Ask me Bryan." But he doesn't. Instead, he just stares at me with his lips parted, surprised. "Dreams are poison. They turn to dust too quickly and infect every part of your life like a cancer that can't be stopped. I refuse to waste my life looking backward Bryan. There's nothing there for me, so tell me why we're reliving the past? Why'd you bring me here?"

Bryan rolls onto his back and breathes. He watches the sky for a long time before taking my hand, and weaving our fingers together. I want to pull away, but it's not because I don't enjoy his touch, but the opposite. Every caress of his skin on mine leaves me craving more.

"Do you hate me?" he finally asks. When I open my mouth to respond, he adds, "Tell me the truth. I'll know if you're lying and I don't need more lies—not from anyone, especially you."

His hand remains holding mine. My first response was to say I don't hate him, but I don't know him anymore. "Bryan, I don't know what to think—of you or this. It seems like you wanted to be with me again, but then I don't understand why you—" My words erupt into a shrill scream when I feel something cold and sharp dig into my ankle. I dart upright, shrieking.

Bryan copies me and looks around for the source of my outcry. A big fat duck is standing by my foot and staring at me like I'm insane. It's right next to me and I had no idea it was there. I'm hysterical and practically crawling my way onto Bryan's lap as the beast honks and steps toward me.

Bryan doesn't know what's happened, but doesn't push me away. His arms close around me and he asks.

"It bit me! Get away!" I'm yelling at the duck and kicking my foot at it.

"Seriously?" He smiles and looks between me and the overly affectionate animal.

"Yes! The fucker frickin bit me!" A few old ladies on the patio gasp at my language, but the duck stands there, licking his chops like he wants more. Frantically, I gesture to my leg and stutter out more phrases, most of which are totally incoherent.

"Calm down. Let me look at it." Bryan tries to pry me off, but I can't let go. That monster is still there, waiting to eat my leg off. I cling to Bryan, digging my nails into his shoulders, and refusing to release him.

I shake my head furiously. "No!"

"Okay, okay," he says softly, not trying to put me down. Somehow he manages to get to his feet and carries me to one of the lawn chairs. The duck stays where we were laying and stares at me, blinking it's beady black eyes. "Let me see your ankle."

I pull up my jean leg and expect to see mangled skin, but there's not even a mark. I blink, not understanding. "But he bit me."

One of the old ladies on the porch is close enough to hear me. She says, "That one is too friendly for his own good. He gave you a little love bite, that's all." She's trying not to laugh, but there's an amused grin on her face.

"A love bite?" Bryan echoes.

She turns to him and nods. "That one must have been a pet. He has two brothers and the three of them usually walk around like they grew up in a bucket, smashed together. My guess is someone got them for Easter and then dumped them at the river when they got too big. This one is too friendly. He wanders up here and goes into the house all the time. He likes her."

I let out a shaky breath and don't know if I should laugh or cry. "I got attacked by a duck." I sound shocked.

"No babe, a duck tried to make out with your ankle. I'll have to try that later." There's laughter in his voice, although he keeps the smile off his face. "You're all right, you know. You'll always be all right. You've been through so much and I'm sure you could kick that duck's ass if you had to." Bryan's lips twitch as he says the last sentence, which is contagious.

Laughter and tears burst through at the same time and I can't stop. Bryan wraps his arms around me and kisses my cheek before wiping away the tears. He holds my face in his hands and looks into my eyes. "The last thing I needed is more competition. Tell me, where do I stand compared to Neil and the ankle biter over there? He's kind of hot, in a Howard the Duck kind of way. You're not into that, are you? I'm only asking because it's been a while."

I manage to elbow him in the ribs and he lets out an *oof* sound. "No! I don't do livestock!"

The old lady on the porch spews her tea and starts choking as the duck takes a step closer. My grip on Bryan loosens before I stand and then stomp my foot at the animal. A normal duck would have run, but that stupid thing just stands there and eyes my foot like it's porn. Bryan laughs as the old lady mops up her table before her tea spills onto her friends.

"Come on, Hallie." Bryan takes my hand and pulls me away. We cut to the path that leads to the parking lot. "It's time to do something I've always wanted, but never had the chance."

Distracted, I glance behind us. The damn duck is following, waddling slowly behind on the path. Two other white ducks emerge from the shrubs and flank him. "Yeah, and what's that?" I ask not really paying attention.

He jerks my arm and pulls me close. My body presses tightly to his and he has my full attention. "I want to taste every inch of you." The look in his eye and the way he holds me tells me that he means it. I part my lips to say something, but he offers another of those light kisses and I forget what I was going to say. The way his lips brush against mine is like a drug, clouding all thoughts, except one—I want more.

CHAPTER 12

It's late afternoon by the time we're at his place—correction—his family mansion. I glance over at him like he's crazy when he pulls his little sports car up into the courtyard. He cuts the engine and gets out, before walking around and opening my door.

As he holds it for me and offers his hand, I tease, "You still live with your mother? Lame." But it's so far from lame that it's not funny. Bryan has his own wing in the estate home. The Ferro fortune is vast and the size of this mansion indicates how deep their pockets extend. My hand slips into Bryan's palm and tingles shoot straight through me. I forget how to breathe.

Bryan offers a smirk as his grip tightens, but it slips away instantly. My statement was so ludicrous that there's no way he should be upset about it, but he seems to be. "Come along, Hallie. No more fighting it or putting it off."

I can't help it. I bait him. "Put what off? I'm not the one who tossed my ass out last night. I was ready to go." I'm such a liar and he knows it.

Bryan rounds on me, his expression formidable, and brings his lips so close to mine that I think he's going to kiss—or bite—me. "Lies are not becoming on you."

"They don't exactly flatter you, either." My heart is beating so loud that I'm sure he can hear it. Why can't I act like he's a jackass? Bryan Ferro is a messed up asshole and yet, I turn to mush when he touches me or flashes those startling green eyes my way. The intensity of his gaze frightens me and I can't hide the tremble it causes.

"I've not lied to you."

"You haven't told me the truth, either. An omission is a lie, so let's not play games."

His eyes dip to my lips. "Fine, then let's do what we came here for."

My heart slams into my ribs by his abruptness. There's no subtle talk, not for him, not this time. "I'm going to take you to my bed, strip you naked, and lick every inch of your beautiful body before making you scream my name as you come. You'll be so sated you won't be able to walk for a week."

My lower lip quivers involuntarily. Bryan closes the space between us and nips my lip before backing away and tugging my arm toward the door. We walk through the mansion, passing servants—all of them ignore us. Suddenly, I'm so nervous that I lose all my muster. He's the one in control and calling the shots.

I've been here before. I've walked these hallways and been in his bed. It's like déjà vu and the emotions hurling through me are a million times worse than last night.

I jerk his arm when we're about to enter his room. "What if your sister sees us?"

"Jos isn't here."

I nod and look at the floor as he reaches for the doorknob. I can't step into those rooms. I'll be pummeled by flashbacks and fall to pieces. "How is she?" Jocelyn is his twin sister and way too nice to be related to any of them. She has dark hair and green eyes, but that's where their similarities end. She has a softness to her that's so innocent, which is weird since she grew up with four Ferro brothers. Add in their deranged cousins and it's the strangest thing I've ever seen.

Bryan shrugs and starts to open the door. "Same as she's always been—too soft." He pauses for a beat, like he's thinking about something. His eyes dip to his hand on the doorknob and I have no idea what he's recalling—if it's about me or another part of his messed up life.

I blurt out, "What about your brothers?"

"They're not here either." Bryan's hand slips off the knob and he turns to look at me. A wicked grin spreads across his lips. "Are you afraid to be here, Hallie? Last time you were in this hallway you practically broke the door down to get at my bed." My face flames red and I try to look away. The memory ignites like dried tinder and I gasp. Bryan takes my chin and turns my face back toward him. "Well?"

"I'm not afraid." My pulse quickens with the lie.

Bryan leans in and whispers in my ear, which shoots an electric current straight into my stomach. My spine stiffens in response and I stop breathing. "Then prove it."

He backs away and his gaze shifts to meet mine. I know when I'm being baited, but my response is juvenile. I can't let him see how weak I've become, and yet, when I walk through that door the things I wrote in my book will become real again. The memories will spring forth and there will be no way to separate them from this and I'll lose whatever joy they brought me.

Shoving past him, I reach for the knob and twist. My heart thumps rapidly like there's a lion on the other side, but I push the door open and walk in. Bryan follows after me and shuts the door behind me. I don't turn, but I hear the lock click.

My eyes wander from one surface to another—the dresser, the bed, the big leather chair, the window sill—and I remember him there and the things he did to me. The sensations flood me, too many of them, all at once. I stand there frozen being barraged by my past, hearing echoes of things that once were and are no more. My jaw locks tight as my ears hear only white noise coupled with the sounds of ancient echoes—Bryan's deep moans of pleasure and the way he'd cry out as he dug his fingers into my hips, driving deeper into me as he did so. I hear voices that no longer exist and feel like I'm trapped in a dream that's crumbling to bits.

I lose my nerve and spin on my heel, darting for the door, but Bryan cuts me off and steps in front of me. He looks down at my face and rests his hands on my shoulders. "A deal is a deal. Don't ruin it now, not when you're almost done."

I don't pretend anymore, I can't. He can't possibly fathom what this place is doing to me, how cruel it is to submerge me in the past this way. I'm drowning in memories that were once happy and now he's tainting them. They're toxic, poisoning me, seeping into my lungs and drowning me.

Run Hallie…run. The voice in my head sounds panicked.

I try to breathe but I can't. The pressure on my ribs is squeezing so tightly that it feels like I'm trapped under a pile of rocks, having every last breath squeezed from my lungs. "STOP!" I scream and pound my fists into his chest, shouting out whatever comes into my mind. "You knew what this would do to me, you knew, and you brought me here anyway!"

"You said yes." His voice is calm, but he grabs my wrists so I can't hit him a second time. He holds me tight and yanks my arms upward, making me look into his eyes. "You had a choice and you willingly came here."

"Don't do this to me."

"I could say the same thing to you, but I haven't. This is a business transaction,

Hallie. There doesn't have to be any emotion, so set yours aside."

"I'm not dead inside, Bryan! I still feel and want things…" I'm breathing hard when my voice trails off. My chest rises and falls like I've been running too far, for too long.

I'm alive.

For the first time in a long time, I feel it, and I know it. I still mourn my life and my losses, but I don't want to wallow there any longer. I want my life back and I want to fight for it. I grit my teeth and rip my wrists from his grasp, not knowing if he's doing this on purpose or if Bryan just brings me back because of who he is—my other half.

From the time I first met him, he had this way about him. Everything from his touch, to the way he thought, lined up and complimented my own. At times I couldn't tell where I ended and he began. I didn't believe in soul mates, until I met him and have seen no evidence of them since. But the world is cruel to match me with him. Bryan Ferro, the heartless.

I repeat, "I'm not dead inside."

His voice is gentler this time, coaxing me out of my fear. "Then prove it, Hallie. I know you've held back so much for so long. Take it out on me. Use me, have me in any way you want—any way you need. Don't think, just act. Take what you need and don't consider tomorrow. Live right here and now. Make a memory that you won't regret." Bryan watches me closely, his eyes scanning my face, looking for signs of my intentions. He's so close to me that the draw to him tugs hard, yanking over and over again to close the distance, but I can't move.

He has to understand, but I know he doesn't. "I never meant to hurt you."

"I know."

"Not back then and not now." He nods slowly, his eyes never leaving mine. I swallow hard waiting for him to say something, but he doesn't. "Do you believe me?"

"The truth?" He presses his lips together and looks away. "I know you didn't mean to, but it still ripped me apart—both times. After all these years, I hear about you from a goddamn book and see you on a fucking stage. Did I mean so little to you that you'd—" He smiles hard, fake, and shakes his head. "No, this is why I chose to do things this way. There's no way around it. The past is the past and there's no future for us—we both know it—so let's stop skirting around the obvious. I want you and you want me. Your current boyfriend hasn't satisfied you since you met. If he did, you would have written about him. So do what comes naturally, Hallie, and be my little slut one more time." His voice becomes cold as he speaks and there's no hint of the warm, playful man I knew.

My hand flies and slaps his cheek. The sound is deafening. My body becomes rigid and for a moment, neither of us moves.

Bryan finally steps aside and unlocks the door. "Your call. You can go back to that idiot or be my sex goddess for the night, but if you go back to him every deal you have on the table will be gone by morning."

I step away from the door, toward him. I'm not thinking about the money or his threats, but something else. "Why didn't you just ask me?"

"Ask you what?"

I tuck my hair behind my ear and spit it out. It's the question that's been bouncing around in my mind since I saw him at the hotel. "Why didn't you just ask me to sleep with you? Why didn't you come up to me after the awards show and invite me to relive old times? Why'd you have to do things this way?"

He laughs once, but there's no happiness in it. "I have my reasons."

"Chicken." I take a step closer to him. I know I'm playing with fire. I don't understand his sudden onset of anger or softness. His mind is a puzzle to me.

"Prude."

I laugh. "We both know that's not true."

"No, we don't. People change, and you've repressed every urge you ever had. I'd be amazed if you could even find my dick, never mind the rest."

My jaw drops, but my shock dissipates and my tongue sharpens. "Asshole."

"You used to like that too." He grins. I shove him with my palms, half laughing, and half serious. This brings a smile to those wicked lips. "So you want it rough?" Pressing my mouth shut, I shake my head. "Then what do you want?"

"To be someone else." I smile grimly. "I'm supposed to be loyal and faithful, even though Neil told me to do this. I'm supposed to be someone else, anywhere else, but here I am with you."

Bryan takes my face in his palms and tilts my head up. He meets my gaze and the surge of lust smashes into me like a tidal wave. He draws my thoughts from me, one at a time. "But you want to be here?" I can't look at him. "And you want things that you shouldn't?"

"Bryan…" I make the mistake of glancing up at him.

His eyes are so vibrant, so green and perfect. His lips are full and the softest shade of pink. I want to lean into his firm chest and press my lips to his. I want to follow the course that my body sets out for us and see where it goes, but I can't. I can't—that phrase—repeats over and over again.

"Hallie, kiss me." His voice has the tone of a command, but I can tell that I have a choice. He won't force me, even though he's threatened to. My gaze fixates on his mouth and I think about how much I want those lips and how desperate I am to taste his kiss.

The problem is that I don't know if this will destroy everything I had with him before. I'm so afraid of losing the only good parts of my past that I'm paralyzed. I can't move forward, but I can't go back. Bryan rubs his thumb along my cheek and whispers, "One kiss, Hallie."

The draw to him, to his lips, is impossible to resist. A kiss won't change things, so I stop fighting it and lean in. My lips brush across his as he cups my face with his hands. It's that light kiss from before, the one that makes me want so much more. By the time he pulls away, I'm gasping and trembling.

Bryan doesn't release me, instead he leans close and kisses my cheek. Currents sizzle through me as I resist the urge to fall into his arms and let him have his way with me. Will it be like it was? That was so long ago. I'm not the same person anymore and neither is he. I'm lost in thought when he says, "Stop thinking." He plants a kiss at the base of my neck and the thoughts blow away like leaves in the wind. My knees buckle and I fall against his firm chest.

Bryan's lips sweep over my neck and are gone too soon. He steps back and takes all the air with him. I nearly stumble forward, but manage to right myself. I hate it when he does that. It makes me want more and suddenly I can see us together for a moment, our two bodies sliding against each other and covered in a sheen of sweat. I gasp at myself. I shouldn't want this with him. He's using me... but then his words bounce back in my mind. He wants me to use him. Can I do that?

Can this just be sex and nothing more? Bryan's face is flushed and he's breathing hard. His eyes are hooded and that hot gaze is lingering on my breasts. "Strip for me, Hallie."

I don't want to do what he says, but my hands move without my consent and I peel off my top and shimmy out of my jeans after shucking my shoes. I'm standing there barefoot wearing nothing but my bra and panties, but that's not good enough. "Lose all of it." Bryan folds his arms across his chest and slips those beautiful eyes over my body before meeting my gaze. "I want you naked, now."

Something about his voice reminds me of old times, but the look in his eyes is different. It's as if he's hungry for me, like he'll never see me again. Reaching around to my back, I unhook my bra and let it slip away. The fabric falls to the floor at his feet as my pulse pounds harder. Every inch of me is tingling, wanting to be touched, but Bryan doesn't move.

"Continue." He says with a look of utter indifference.

I'm standing there wondering what the hell I'm doing. I could grab my clothes and run or give in. The logical part of my mind is telling me to run like hell, but I don't. My feet stay glued before him, half naked. Bryan's eyes lift from my breasts to meet my gaze. We watch each other as I make my decision. Memories of him fly by beneath my eyelids—kisses, touches, and things too intimate to do with anyone else—things carnal by nature. Bryan never judged me for that and in that moment, I want him so much that I can't stand it. The pull to him is so intense, so illogical. The door behind me is unlocked and the windows aren't shaded. Anyone could see me and yet, I don't care.

I loved him once. It took so long to get over him.

You never got over him, the voice in my head chides.

Just breathe. My thumbs hook into the sides of my panties and I slip them past my hips and down my thighs. I loop the little lacy fabric over my foot and step toward Bryan, handing them to him the way I'd done in the past. He hides his emotions, but acts the way he used to. He lifts my bottoms to his nose and inhales deeply, closing his eyes as he does so. When those green orbs open again, he watches me through lowered lashes and tucks my panties into his pocket. "On the bed."

I want to see him and run my fingertips over his slick skin, but Bryan doesn't strip. I glance at the door and back at him. He offers a smirk. "Worried about getting caught?"

"No," I lie, trying to be more confident than I actually am. "What about you?"

"Hell no. I'd be proud if someone caught me with you." That makes me smile, I can't help it. I try to hide it by turning around and padding across the room to his bed. It's a huge room, with a sitting area and a media room off to both sides, but the bed is across from the door at the back of the room.

Bryan has an antique four poster bed. The posts are carved swirls that spire up high into the room. The walls are painted to look like leather and his blankets are different than the last time I was here, more mature. They're dark browns and blacks, sophisticated and expensive. "Crawl up."

I do as he says, expecting him to tell me to turn, but he grabs my bare hips and stops me. "Stay like that and let me taste you." Bryan leans in and before I feel his mouth, his warm breath passes over my sensitive parts. I shudder and try not to gasp, but I already did. When his tongue

THE PROPOSITION 2

licks my seam and pushes deeper I fight the sensations shooting through me. It's been so long since I was kissed this way. Bryan is gentle at first, but then he laps me, drinking me like he could never get enough. His tongue pushes deeper and he pulls my hips back, encouraging me to rock against him. After more delicious licks, I'm still stiff.

Bryan lifts his head. "Relax and enjoy it. Let go, Hallie. I won't hurt you. I promise."

False promises. The thought rings in my head before his mouth goes back to work.

Every pass of his tongue makes me lose more and more of myself until I'm surrounded in a cloud of lust, unable to find my way out. I press back into his mouth as he darts his tongue deeper into my folds. My hands splay on the bed and I rest my head, leaving my hips in the air so he can have his way with me. I buck into him, feeling things I haven't felt in forever. I'm burning, demanding, and begging him to push me over the edge of ecstasy.

I'm not Hallie anymore—I'm his. I want him to do anything and everything. I beg him for it, saying things that I haven't said before, but he doesn't stop. Instead, Bryan flicks, sucks, and teases me until I'm promising him anything. "That's the Hallie I know. Keep begging me baby, and I'll be good to you."

Bryan dips his head once more and his tongue is so warm—so perfect. He touches me gently as his fingers push into me, rubbing the perfect spot until I find my release. I cry out, pushing back into his face before I go still. My heart continues to pound violently as Bryan licks me until he's satisfied. His touches are tender and so different from the last time we were together.

Between breaths, my hazy thoughts whisper nonsense about love and gentle caresses. For a second I wonder if he got over me. He's not said a thing about it and his actions are so bipolar that this could be a whim.

Perhaps Bryan heard about me on the television and wanted me again. Maybe he's between lovers and thought it would be easier to blackmail me rather than find a new girlfriend. No, that doesn't sound like him. Bryan could flash that beautiful smile at any woman and her knees would weaken. He came after me for a reason, and although he acts like it's revenge, this didn't feel like it. It felt soft and pure—two traits that Bryan is normally lacking.

Bryan is still clothed when he crawls up on the bed beside me. He sits on the edge, next to me, watching. His eyes linger on my bare curves. It makes me wish he'd wrap his arms around me. Pretending doesn't sound so bad right now. If it were years ago, I'd roll into his arms and he'd kiss me senseless until I was ready to keep going, but that's not the way things go tonight.

When he speaks his voice sounds labored. "Roll over so I can see you." I do as he asked, even though I feel shy about it. It's been years since he's seen me. My hips aren't small and my thighs are way past thin. My curves have filled out, and not in ways desirable to me. Neil encourages me to work out, but I haven't—not since I lost my father.

Bryan's hot gaze lingers on my hips, before traveling up to my neck, and then resting on my face. He smiles thoughtfully.

Softly he says, "I had no idea beauty intensifies with age. This curve right here is perfection." He presses his finger to the base of my hip and draws a line up to my waist. I suck in a breath, but try to be still. Every time he touches me, I crave more. It's as if the boundaries that divide the present and the past have crumbled. I don't care why I'm here at this moment, I just want things to be the way they were before he left me.

Bryan scoots up to the headboard and lies back on his pillows before patting the spot next to him. I follow his silent directive and crawl to the empty space beside him. Bryan wraps an arm around me and pulls me to his side.

I refuse to think. I will not be overcome with the onslaught of emotions that this small gesture brings. As we lay together, his breathing slows and I know he's fallen asleep. When I listen to him breathe, I hear that hitch—that small gasp of air—that was there when we were in his hotel room. I didn't imagine it. Is he crying in his sleep? What's causing that sound? It's heartbreaking to listen to.

I remain by his side for an hour or more. By the time I push up, it's dark and Bryan shows no sign of rousing. Pushing up on my elbow, I look down at his serene face and brush the dark hair from his brow. I whisper to him things that I probably shouldn't say, but life's too short to go on like this. "I missed you so much. I wish things were different. I wish you were still mine."

CHAPTER 13

I head into his bathroom—it's bigger than my Dad's house—and try to fix my hair. It's all mussed like I was doing naughty things. If his mother is home, I'll die. I open a drawer looking for a comb or something to smooth down my frizzy fro when I see a plethora of little orange prescription bottles. They roll to the front of the drawer making it easy to see the name typed on the stickers: BRYAN FERRO.

I lift one and look at it. I don't recognize the drug, but some of the others are familiar. Bottle after bottle of pain killers, mostly narcotics, fill the drawer. I glance back at Bryan, asleep on the bed, and wonder what he's gotten himself into. He's a pill junkie? I couldn't even tell he was on anything.

The spot in the center of my chest feels hollow with this revelation. The Bryan I knew didn't mess around with drugs, but this man does. I wonder what else he does, what other forms of entertainment he partakes of that are foreign to me.

I close the drawer and open another, finally finding a brush. I run it through my hair and do the best I can given the state my hair is in. I tidy up my smeared make-up and decide that's the best it's going to get.

The question of how to get home is still reeling through my mind. I need to get to Maggie still and convince her to stay with me and Neil tonight. Neil. That's going to be weird. I shove aside the thoughts and tiptoe past Bryan and out his door, quietly closing it behind me.

When I turn around, I smack into a firm chest and look up. Jon Ferro, Bryan's cousin, is standing there with a bemused look on his face.

As soon as he recognizes me his happy expression shifts to anger. "What are you doing here?" Jon is all muscle, dark hair, and bright blue eyes like his brothers. He's my least favorite person to talk to, so I try to walk past him, but he grabs my elbow. "Don't tell me he's gotten back together with you."

God, I hate him. My eyes narrow into slits and I tug my arm away. "Do not touch me." My voice is steady, low, and even. "And he's asleep so don't be your normal dickish self and wake him up."

Jon glances at the door with a confused expression. By the time he looks back for me, I'm hurrying down the hallway. *Don't follow me. Don't follow me. Don't follow me.* I chant the words inside my head, but they do no good. Actually, they appear to do the opposite, because Jon chases after me and falls in step at my side. "You know you're not wanted here."

"Yeah, I know." I hurry ahead, trying to get out the door before Jocelyn or the rest of Bryan's family sees me. They can't stand me, but I have no idea why. Bryan's the one who broke up with me. I should be insignificant and forgotten.

"Then, why'd you come?"

I stop abruptly and look at the guy. He has no clue what Bryan did to me, how he showed up and turned my life upside down. "Bryan didn't give me much of a choice and now that I'm trying to leave, you won't let me. What do you want Ferro?" I fold my arms over my chest like I'm tough shit, but I'm shaking inside.

Jon studies me for a moment, looking for lies, before asking, "How'd you get here?"

"Bryan drove me."

"How are you leaving?"

"No idea. Probably walking until I can get my friend to pick me up."

Jon laughs at that. "You can't walk. Some drunk movie star will smear your ass across the pavement." I continue walking, ready to shove out the front door, when Jon grabs my arm again. "Hallie, wait—and don't go that way. Aunt Lizzy is out there and you know how she is, perpetually pissed. Come around back. You can take my car. I'll get it from you later after I slap some sense into my idiot cousin."

He releases me and I follow after him. I want to protest, but I'm not waking up Bryan to ask for a ride home. Besides, he shouldn't be driving if he's doped up out of his freaking mind. I glance at Jon, who is one of Bryan's best friends and blurt it out because I have to know how far Bryan's fallen since I've seen him last. "Do you guys party like you used to? Or did your choice in entertainment mature over the past few years?"

Jon's face scrunches up as he looks over his shoulder at me. "What the hell are you talking about?"

"Nothing." I'm sorry I asked. Jon gives me another look, but doesn't let it drop.

"If you have a question, ask it."

"Do you guys party hard? Drugs? Hookers? Ya know, stuff like that?"

Jon lurches to a stop and spins on his heel. He looks down at me with an expression that I can't read. "Is this because of Trystan Scott?"

"No." That was a weird response. Why would I ask about a rock star?

Jon shakes his head slightly and lets out an annoyed breath. "Bryan's clean. He doesn't dip his dick where he shouldn't, and keeps his nose clean. The worst stuff the guy does is usually with me and Scott, which involves alcohol and a vast amount of stupidity." He smirks, "But Bryan's funny as hell—smashed or not." Jon's smile fades and his eyes cut back to me. "Why'd you ask?"

I lie. "No reason."

Jon rolls his eyes. "Whatever. I'll find out eventually and if it stems back to you—"

My eyes narrow and my voice steels. I mean every word I say. "I wouldn't hurt him."

"Yeah. Whatever." He doesn't believe me. We're at the back of the house and I follow Jon outside to his little red car.

When I get closer I can tell what it is and smile. "You're driving a chick car."

Jon shoots me an evil look as he hands me the key fob. "Yeah, courtesy of my mother and her attempts to emasculate me. Do me a favor and park it in the 'hood and leave the keys on the seat. You live in a rough part of town, right?" He grins at me and slips his hands into his pockets.

"You want me to take your car so it gets stolen?" He nods. "Pampered ass." I grumble and open the door before sliding into the driver's seat.

Jon pushes the door shut. "I have to get rid of it. Do you have a better suggestion?"

I start the engine. "Uh, yeah. Sell it like a normal person."

"Fine, you have tits—you want it?" Jon's being crass trying to get under my skin.

I laugh at him. "I have no money, smart ass."

"But you will, right? How about this, ten grand and it's yours—or park it someplace horrible and let the thing get stolen. You pick."

Ten grand? Is he mental? "The car is brand new. The sticker price had to be close to fifty thousand—this thing is loaded."

"Again, so?" I consider it for a moment. I need a car and I could spend ten grand of my advance to get this one. I was going to get an old Honda. A new Miata would be way cooler. Jon grins when he knows he has me hooked. "Drop off a check whenever you get around to it. The title is in the glove box."

Jon starts to walk away, but I call out to him. "Hey! Does Bryan usually fall asleep this early?"

Jon turns and watches me for a moment before shaking his head. "No, maybe you wore him out. Oh, and in case I wasn't clear—stay away from him. He has enough shit going on without you reappearing."

I laugh and drive away muttering, "If you only knew."

CHAPTER 14

There's a satisfied smile on my lips when I walk up the front porch. Between Bryan and the car, today didn't turn out half bad, well, except for the random duck attack. I must be mental, because I'm happy about being blackmailed for sex and excited about getting played into buying a car. Since I do in fact have boobs—they're a pretty good pair, actually—the little red car is perfect for me.

When I shove open the front door, I'm shocked to see Cecily. She's sitting on the couch next to Neil. They both stand and Cecily rushes toward me and takes my hands, jabbering about the contracts. I nod at them and look around for Maggie, but don't see her.

I cut off Cecily. "I'm sorry, one second. Neil, where is Maggie?"

"She ran out for a little bit. She said she'd be here when you got back, but she's running late." Neil has a look on his face like he's proud of me for taking one for the team, but there's a lingering of disgust dusting his expression as well. When Cecily starts talking again, his eyes cut to her.

Cecily pulls me toward the couch. "Sit, sit. We've been waiting for you. I have the contracts right here. This one is for the book and this is the movie option. The contracts to purchase the rights are already in motion, this is just a formality—and more money." She points at clauses and explains what they mean before flipping to the final page and handing me a pen. "This is it, Hallie. Sign right here and get ready for your life to change. Everything you ever wanted and more will come flooding your way."

I stare at the papers knowing that this is a life altering moment. Neil is beaming at me, as if he were proud, but deep down he must be resentful, right? He said all that stuff about working hard for his living, and I earned mine from sex and luck. I shouldn't feel guilty about it. This should be a happy day for me, one of the best days of my life.

Swallowing hard, I scrawl my name across both contracts and shove them back at her. "Done. When can I expect to see that money?"

Cecily laughs as she takes the papers and puts them in her briefcase. "It'll be a while before the first payment comes in. I could spot you a little bit for now. What do you need?" She reaches for a checkbook, and pauses, waiting for me to answer.

How much do I need? Everything. Enough to move, save Maggie, and pay for my car. Before I can say anything, Neil cuts me off. "She doesn't need anything. I'll take care of her, but thank you." The two of them exchange a look that has too many secret smiles. Cecily backs away toward the door, giving Neil plenty of space. I'm still sitting on the couch and Neil is standing in front of me.

He slips his hands into his pockets and smiles down at me. "I'm so proud of you, Hallie. You've been through so much and you came through it more radiant than ever. There are few women who have the strength you have, and even fewer who would do anything to please the man they love. You are the right woman for me, the best companion, lover, and friend that I could ever hope for."

Neil goes down on one knee at the same time he pulls a ring from his pocket. He holds out a golden band with a huge diamond mounted in the center. My jaw drops open, as shock steals my breath when he asks, "Will you marry me?"

COMING SOON:

THE PROPOSITION VOL 3

To ensure you don't miss the next installment, text AWESOMEBOOKS to 22828 and you will get an email reminder on release day.

*****

THE FERRO BROTHER MOVIE

Vote now to make it happen!
http://www.ipetitions.com/petition/ferro/

*****

What do you think Hallie will say?
Go to Facebook.com/HMWard and join the discussion!

*****

MORE FERRO FAMILY BOOKS

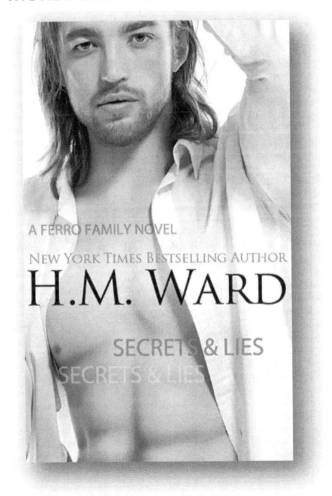

SECRETS & LIES

BRYAN FERRO
~THE PROPOSITION~

*****

SEAN FERRO
~THE ARRANGEMENT~

******

PETER FERRO GRANZ
~DAMAGED~

******

JONATHAN FERRO
~STRIPPED~

MORE ROMANCE BOOKS BY

H.M. WARD

DAMAGED

THE ARRANGEMENT

STRIPPED

SCANDALOUS

SCANDALOUS 2

SECRETS

THE SECRET LIFE OF TRYSTAN
SCOTT

And more.

To see a full book list, please visit:

www.SexyAwesomeBooks.com/books.htm

CAN'T WAIT FOR H.M WARD'S NEXT STEAMY BOOK?

Let her know by leaving stars and
telling her what you liked about
THE PROPOSITION VOL. 2
in a review!